For my daughter, Mikaela.

With many thanks to my husband, Jared,
for all of his support and encouragement.

First paperback edition June 2022.

ISBN 979-8-9858462-0-1 (Hardcover)
ISBN 979-8-9858462-1-8 (Paperback)
ISBN 979-8-9858462-2-5 (eBook)

Published by Damselfly Reads
www.damselflyreads.com

BIG THINGS

a STORY FOR OLDER SiBLiNGS of C-BABieS

Written by
Danielle L. Forbes

Illustrations by
Anastasiia Bielik

Today is the big day!
Mommy, Daddy and our new baby
are home from the hospital.
We are a big brother and a big sister now!

Our new baby came out of Mommy's belly.
Now her belly has a boo-boo.
We must be very gentle with her
until the boo-boo gets better.

The boo-boo is not our baby's fault.
Sometimes boo-boos happen.

Just like when we get boo-boos
while we are playing.

While Mommy's belly hurts, she cannot pick us up.
We are too heavy for right now.
But we can do something our new baby is
too small to do- we can hold her hand!

When we are excited, can Mommy pick us up?
No, Mommy's belly hurts.
But we can give her high fives or do a little dance
with her. She still loves to have fun with us.

When we are sad, can Mommy pick us up?
No, Mommy's belly hurts. But we can sit
next to her for hugs and kisses. She will
always want to make us feel better.

Mommy says her boo-boo is not forever.
She will be able to pick us up again
when her boo-boo is all gone.

She also says we are a big brother and a
big sister now and we can do...

BIG THINGS!

Because we are a big boy and a big girl now, we can help clean up. When we play with our toys, we can put them away after we are done playing with them. That way Mommy can rest.

Because we are a big boy and a big girl now,
we can help by reading stories and singing
songs to our new baby.

Our new baby loves to hear our voices. They know we are their big brother and big sister. Our new baby loves us a lot.

Mommy and Daddy love us very much, too.
Mommy's boo-boo on her belly and
our new baby do not change that.

Our parents are very proud of us because we are a big brother and a big sister now and we can do...

BIG THINGS!

For more resources to
support your C-Mama and littles
during these BIG family transitions,
please go to www.damselflyreads.com.

Please review
BIG THINGS: A Story for Older Siblings of C-Babies on Amazon!

Made in United States
Orlando, FL
12 May 2024